Daisy

Daisy

POEMS

Rachel Feder

TriQuarterly Books / Northwestern University Press

EVANSTON, ILLINOIS

TriQuarterly Books
Northwestern University Press
www.nupress.northwestern.edu

Printed in the United States of America

10 9 8 7 6 5 4 3 2 1

LIBRARY OF CONGRESS CATALOGING-IN-PUBLICATION DATA
Names: Feder, Rachel, author.
Title: Daisy : poems / Rachel Feder.
Description: Evanston, Illinois : TriQuarterly Books / Northwestern University Press, 2025.
Identifiers: LCCN 2024048656 | ISBN 9780810148352 (paperback) | ISBN 9780810148369 (ebook)
Subjects: LCGFT: Poetry.
Classification: LCC PS3606.E333 D35 2025 | DDC 811/.6—dc23/eng/20241105
LC record available at https://lccn.loc.gov/2024048656

For Moshe, with love

CONTENTS

Erasure:
The Great Gatsby, First Chapter

I am still a little afraid of missing something

I wanted the world to be riotous
an unbroken series of gestures

there was something gorgeous about romantic readiness
the wake of dreams abortive and short-winded

hard-boiled I came back
restless, the warm center of the world

Why—ye-es
I had just left
I went alone
I ran away

On the road I was lonely, a pathfinder
just as things grow fast I had so much to be pulled down
in red and gold like new money from the mint, promising
to unfold the shining secrets

I was rather literary
I was going to bring back the body
not perfect like a wingless phenomenon

I lived a superficial, sinister contrast
My raw ivy and marble
I had a view of the water, glittered

along the water
in bright vines glowing now with reflected gold

his legs apart
straw-haired
the enormous power of that body, glistening
muscle shifting

a cruel body
a gruff touch
and while we were never intimate he approved of me, turning
me around by the arm, fragile and gleaming
white against the fresh grass
wine-colored shadow

two young women in white groan, completely motionless

Daisy laughed, an absurd, charming little laugh, and I laughed too and came

up and down is an arrangement, her face
was sad and lovely with bright things in it
bright eyes and a bright passionate mouth

Do they miss me?
The whole town is desolate.
I enjoyed looking at her.

Slenderly, languidly, their hands
set lightly on their hips, the two young women open
toward the sunset, where candles flicker

Daisy snapped her little finger
black and blue

silver

silver

glowing

then the glow faded

some woman

some woman

a nightingale

I remember the candles

being lit again, a shrill metallic urgency

of twilight

I woke out of the ether and bloomed with light

Daisy

Just a Girl

When I turn the doorknob,   I come out
                                        of myself for a moment,

like letting fireflies out of a jar.   I see a girl.
    She walks into her room and sucks the air into her like a black hole.

She walks into the room and takes up the right amount of space.
    She takes off her bra,   pulls off her velvet necklace,   lets down

her hair.   At her desk, she takes the phone off its cradle   the phone
    translucent plastic   rainbow wires.   She listens

to its atonal hum   and thinks about the busy signal   if anybody calls.
    She turns on her desk lamp   uncool   her father's   an old
        banker's lamp

a lamp that leans over itself   its leaded glass
                        making a green light in the window.

The Nelson School

~~You would only call it camp in retrospect—~~
~~looking back, we were so young~~
~~at the time we felt like astronauts touching~~
~~down on a distant planet~~

Cuban oregano, the cook's son said
kneeling down outside the art barn

he'd grown up at the school,
only one year older than me

& already I felt him stitching my heart back together.
Tom was back in East Egg, interning for our dads
my destiny back home, my mother's pearls

so tightly knotted around her neck & still
too loose for mine. *Tom.* His eyes, robin's egg
blue, my definition of purity no matter

where he touched me no matter if he was rough or gentle.
But here was something different. Had I been torn
without knowing it, without noticing the damage.

Cuban oregano, he told me
& spoke of its potency he told me it was medicine,

the leaves pungent, crushed against the soil beneath his hand.

Jordyn

Three pebbles against the window, the oak tree carries her
in effortlessly, her arm tangling

in the curtain. *Jordyn* my T-shirt is tight against my body,
my muscles have just started to relax *you look a wreck*

her makeup is smudged down her face—Urban Decay
mascara & loose glitter eye shadow. *I haven't been home*

since this time yesterday she laughs, sweeping her raven curls
unruly over her shoulder. My mother calls Jordyn's parents

permissive. She calls them *new money* which is code for Jewish.
I call Jordyn the only girl I've ever kissed, one night in her dorm

at Nelson after she broke up with her first boyfriend, again
in the stairwell before a party. *It's funny I was just writing*

a poem about the Nelson School, I say looking at the rip in her jeans
& she says *me or him? Wait, don't answer that*. I love Jordyn mostly

because she would never tell Tom any of this, Tom who still thinks
I'm a virgin, that my body is his to take sometime in the heady nights

between senior prom and graduation, whenever he deems
it necessary. Jordyn sees a shadow cross my face

in the green lamplight. *Stop*, she tells me. *You'll just tell him it happened*
horseback riding, and anyway maybe it's time for new material,

the Nelson School was two summers ago & I don't think professors
want to read about your arts program in your portfolio,

isn't that, like, too "meta" or something? She picks at the white threads
where the denim stretches across her knee *and anyway aren't you going*

to ask me where I was?

Sundays

There's a small college in West Egg, across the water.
My parents speak of *town & gown conflict. Liberal arts,*

liberal farts, they say. A small school, a good school,
I've heard, but nonetheless a campus that smells

of ganja, a campus where Phish & DMB blare
from dorm windows. West Egg is dappled

with the same Victorians but they've gone
to seed, prayer flags hanging from the windows

& old sofas on porches. We go there to party.
When I say *we* I exempt myself. Mama & Daddy

are pretty strict with me. No West Egg boys,
no wine from a box. Cotillion, tennis, Tom.

Tom goes, I know it, though he's never said,
to the house parties in West Egg and farther west, too,

to the city. Jordyn sees him. Jordyn is dating Gretchen,
a sophomore political science major who lives in a student co-op.

On Sundays after church I go with her & Gretch makes a hash
of yams & spinach & breaks eggs on top. I wouldn't say

I'm jealous, exactly, but I don't say much. Sunday
is family dinner at our place with Tom and his parents

not prepared by my mother but served by her & Tom's mother
is not to know but suspects, I think, & jousts with her

about the particularities of *gratin* while the fathers pour
another drink & talk shop about the firm & the mothers

scold them *now no more shop talk, boys.* The plan
is Providence next year, everyone's agreed,

Brown for Tom & RISD for me, then marriage
after graduation, then Wharton

while I *get my sea legs*, as my mother puts it,
then Tom will join our fathers' investment firm in the city.

Our daughter the writer, as if it were a charming peculiarity,
as if short of finding a suitably prestigious art school

in Providence it were more or less tangential to the plan.
Of course you'll get in, dear, when they've no reason to of course it.

The Buchanans have been at Brown for generations so of course but
that's not how art school works, Daddy & he adjusts his glasses

that's how everything works, pumpkin and in my head I say no,
no, no. If I get in I want it to be on my own merit but

who am I to talk about merit? What was I doing

that summer, anyway? Working on my manuscript?

Love

Me & Him Him & Me
Thomas my Tom & Daisy myself
like a key to a lock & the lock itself
Growing up together late-night calls *has*
your dad been home *has yours* Summers
in the Hamptons vs. winters in Aspen
wish I had your dad, Daze hot sand
hot hands *your dad shouldn't talk*
to you like that, Tom & *that boy*
is like a son to me you know
that, Daisy they hand
the firm to him I
give him my
hand my
self

The Nelson School (II)

By winter it was a pretty typical prep school, albeit
one that sprawled across a Vermont dairy farm

& the remote setting & "real chores" component
made it a magnet for wealthy parents afraid

of what their precious offspring might otherwise
get up to. He was the poorest kid at school by far,

though ~~ironically~~ it most belonged to him. Summers
the clover thicketed across the lawn & the school

transformed into an arts program, classical oboe
startling the ducks on the pond. Jordyn went every year,

wasn't too worried about her résumé, always assumed
she'd go to college in West Egg and commute from home,

& come senior year her folks already acted like this was the case,
letting her be & breathe & when things went very wrong

at a frat house she spared them the story because *why*
give them guilt over trusting me when it was my own mistake

to be there at that hour and in that dress? So it was dance one summer,
ceramics the next, always a new exploration, the long afternoons

spent in a work-study down at the barn because *new money* or no,
there wasn't as much of it as my mother assumed

just on account of their being here and there being any. So
she mucked stalls & baled hay & ran the curry comb in its insistent

circles, circles that reminded me of a mind racing but seemed to calm
her down, picked hooves & washed saddles & smelled

like a honeyed piece of leather soap. She convinced me to join her
the summer after sophomore year, *come on, Daze, what harm can it do?*

And my parents figured it couldn't hurt to have it on my applications.
She invited me to come again last summer but of course I turned her down.

I was afraid of what else I might do.

Kiss

Nostalgia, the texture of attachment: Say a Halloween party. Say
        Christmas morning. Tom's lips
on mine are just lips, human lips. I'd thought a kiss
        would be something more
than bodies colliding. I thought I'd see stars.
        But I learned. Boy did I learn. He knew me
inside & out, learned me inside & out, knows me
        better than I know myself. Our fathers
in the city working late, our mothers pouring another,
        just one more. Plastic glow-in-the-dark
stars he hung over my bed, standing on the blanket.

Brunch

A poem for you, Nick Carraway, a cousin I've never met
doesn't even know I go by Daisy *and you must be Margaret*

I almost don't correct him because why be known by him?
What is owed to him? Is it possible the St. Paul air hangs

around him, cold and boring? *I go by Daisy,*
and of course my boyfriend Tom and Tom puts his hand

firmly on my knee as if righting a wobbly café table.
And how has your transition been, dear? Mama asks,

then orders another mimosa as the restaurant buzzes
with post-church East Egg and hungover West Egg

Nick you are literally so boring there is nothing to write
a poem about & Tom cracks a joke about the news

& wipes a spot of yolk from my upper lip & in these moments
I remember I love him. *So what are you studying?* He fixes

his gaze on Nick, he has the college lingo down, in high school
you do *homework*, in college you *study* & when Nick says *undecided*

I stifle a giggle & Tom squeezes my knee

& we are in this together. Daddy jumps in with something

about internships after freshman year & post-graduation
job placements & Nick is rapt attention while Tom slides

his thumb up and down against the inside of my knee, cracking
me open like an egg. *Oh my gosh!* Jordyn & Gretchen

at the door, Gretch braless and easy, Jordyn
with a streak of comb-in purple waxy

against her thick curl. *Jordyn what an inventive*
look, my mother compliments, scandalized,

& once they've taken their table for two
by the window Tom pushes a lock

of my hair behind my ear & quips
I dunno, I think you'd look good

with your tips dyed pink, Margaret.

Waiting

g o o d
i r
r e
l a
C m
L
E
A
N
[pure] & [sweet]
I
I
I

I'm a good girl I'm a good girl I'm a good girl I'm a good girl

I will wait for love or at least marriage

Parties

I have this neighbor we're walking Nick back to his dorm
in West Egg my mother's shoes clacking

against brick *he throws these crazy parties. Big old house*
behind my dorm I don't think he has roommates Tom's

alongside Nick both a half-pace ahead of me *No*
roommates? His parents must be loaded & Nick shrugs

I don't really have a sense of him, he's my age but not a student
not sure exactly what he does for work but he moved in this summer

& the house is falling apart but these ragers, dude. You have to come out
& Tom asks *pretty sweet?* & Nick says *well I haven't gone yet*

like he's not a student do I need to wait to be invited &
Tom grunts *your mom's waiting to be invited!*

I can see the house through the alley behind the dorm
white peeled paint & a wrap-around deck

& a beer pong table in the yard & for some reason
a statue of a lion? *That's the place* Nick whispers,

jutting his thumb *you wanna come out sometime*
& Tom says *totally, man. Totally* & I can tell

he means it *but I dunno, man* wrapping his arm
around me as if just remembering I'm there

Margaret here's not much of a party girl.

Sage

Treasure chest on my closet floor reminding me how I love you, why
dance corsages textbook-pressed a plastic ring
you bought from a machine,
sliding the coins in, the crowd an eruption when you bent
down & mock-proposed, how the children cheered & only we knew
it was true and not true, it was a promise
& I keep my promises

the malachite bracelet from the hippy store where we lingered
after we drove Jordyn to the dry cleaner so her mother
wouldn't see

what had happened to her dress the way she couldn't stop shaking &
she said

you guys are so lucky & I knew we were, Tom

I knew we were the lucky ones

& she bought sage & candles & moonstone

& a thin rope bracelet with white beads
you make a wish on each & when they fall off the wishes come true

& the white ones stand for hope or purity or milk
I can't remember

~~why I love you sometimes but I have these tokens & of course~~

~~with you in your father's house & me in mine~~

~~how can we think straight — how can *we* be *us*~~

like beads yoked together   or slivers of malachite

broken from the stone
found in the earth
lying on the path
the path to where we're going

Honey

His father taught him how to harvest honey,
golden mesh across his face. Mixed

with butter from the farm & bread hot
from the oven, it was the most delicious

thing I'd ever tasted. It made me want
to taste everything. I'm just saying

it plain. This is a terrible poem.
Nights I look at the amaryllis

on my windowsill & the translucent
spider who lives there & think

about all that was grown there & all
that was kept alive. Watching

the lunar eclipse on a blanket behind
the art barn, how it turned into a ruddy

red ball & he said *my mother says the moon*
reveals our shadows but everything was dark

& the cicadas sang. What had been illuminated
burst red and *our shadow is covering the moon*

I said & *look our shadow!* he said & he quoted Kerouac,
she brooded and bit her rich lips: my soul began

its first sink into her, deep, heady, lost; like drowning
in a witches' brew, Keltic, sorcerous, starlike &

I said *Jay*, I said it with all the breath I had left,
as our noses touched & he said *let me*

Tragic Kingdom

Get into it, please! Jordyn's singing along
her breathy second soprano layering

over Gwen Stefani's voice in a pleasing
cacophony

something about being just
a girl & what else in the world could we be

I'm stripped
down to my lace trainers

my khakis & striped sweater on her bed *my parents*
will literally murder me if they find out

Well she's affixing Velcro gems to her wild
mane *there's a lot of things they'd kill you about*

so add this to the list & as if to drive her point
home she gives me a chaste peck

on the lips *come on Gretchen is going to be here*
in twenty minutes, plus I told you I saw Nick

last time why should the guys have all the fun?
She pulls a baby doll dress out of her closet,

lace & the palest bunting blue, then eases it over
my head and down around my hips. *Honey.*

Makes a crown of my hair with a swarm
of plastic butterflies, leaving locks

hanging down like a philodendron. Cream
blush, brown mascara, chunky Mary Jane

heels with bubblegum-pink soles. Doorbell.
Mom we're going with Gretchen if Daisy's

parents call but she's cut off *You went*
to Starbucks for a hot cocoa break, got it!

Jordyn brought the CD & pulls it out
its quicksilver bottom sending sparks

around the car *Excuse me mister!* &
there's no going back now.

Purity

Tom knows me inside & out

but with Jay I was a princess in disguise, ripped

jeans & my mother's old polos, not my name, not

my parents, not my house not my money, just me, just me sun-

warmed & honeyed &

burnt like an offering, the bees, the wasps landing on me & glancing

away, just me

there in the sweetness ~~of my own anonymity~~, just my purest self, my only

self, my self

like the grass green at the Nelson School ~~& fresh-cut but by whom~~

& he loved me, he loved that version of me with nothing

but my trunk, nothing to give.

It was the first time I felt pure. That's why I did it.

Glasses Girl

I see her the moment I walk in, leaning
against the wall by the bathroom, talking

to a group of boys. She's unlike anyone
I've ever seen, like a photo in *Twist* magazine.

There is something for my poetry I think, but I can't
pin her down, even now, except maybe the glasses,

large tortoiseshell, like an old man's, while everyone
else is barefaced or, at most, making a move

with skinny black frames. Jordyn & Gretchen
fold into the crowd like chocolate into batter.

Her hair is back in one large clip, a simple
French twist, the clip dappled brown

like the glasses. *Daisy, you came!* my cousin
at my elbow. *You look really nice. Is Tom*

here this time & it's a jagged pill
to swallow, his *this time.*

Was Tom here last time? But his face
has already blanched with the answer.

He tries again. *Can I get you a drink?*
I shake my head, causing the largest

butterfly to flap its metal wings.
I'm overdressed, I know. I glance

again toward Glasses Girl but she's
moved on. *I shouldn't* I say. *So where's*

this crazy neighbor of yours? Nick shrugs,
incredulous. *Would you believe I haven't*

seen him? & I was one of the first people
here. No surprise there, I think,

though I'm feeling unfashionably late,
& where is Jordyn? *I'm going to find the bathroom,*

I say, & he gestures behind him & to the left,
though of course I already know where it is.

I make my way, my arms crossed. Door's
unlocked so I push it open. *Oh, sorry!*

Glasses Girl turns off the sink, unfazed, turns
to face me. Long-sleeved sweater dress, bare

legs, platform sneakers, red flannel shirt
tied around her waist. For a moment

I think I recognize the shirt but then
there's something about her, a gravity

alien & familiar at the same time. She turns
back to the mirror, uncaps a pale pink lip

gloss, applies it to her pout, her nails
a crackled white over blue. *Hey*, she says

when she's finished, as if we've known
each other for ages, *she's all yours*. I shift

my weight to let her out. *I like your glasses*,
I say, finally. She taps the heavy frames.

Thanks. They were my grandfather's. Just
switched out the prescription.

Cool, I say stupidly. *Yeah* she laughs
sometimes it creeps me out like, is Grandpa

watching everything I do from the great beyond?
I laugh too *but I like to think he's watching over*

me she chuckles again & spreads her fingers
ooh, got a little deep there! & she's gone

I struggle the door shut, its bad latch
I pull the butterflies out of my hair

one by one, smudge my makeup
free my bra straps from the capped

sleeves of the dress the bass
is pumping but to be honest

I don't know what to do at a party
head out & find Nick *hey*

sorry can you drive me home?

Shift

August opens her belly to the sky //

I climb into Tom's car //

the summer a secret, a scab, a scar between us //

Tom do I tell him do I not tell him do I tell him do I tell him or not //

I'm as bad as our fathers //

but then he's been with them in the city all summer, training //

grooming, being groomed to take over their investment firm //

his destiny //

I picture him on a car phone shouting *liquidate! liquidate!* //

don't really understand what Daddy does but Tom probably does by now //

& do I tell him I mean do I confess it //

the moment I wonder I realize I was never going to //

realize that was a summer just for me //

but his face // *Tom* // something's shifted // *Tom tell me* //

& he does but not in words I know //

something about the firm //

something about our fathers //

something happened between them //

does he know what? //

He says he doesn't know but do I believe him? //

I don't understand, Tom. My father holds the controlling shares now what does
that mean? //

Means I'm set to inherit the whole company // the Buchanans will be cut
out //

But that firm should be yours, Tom // squeezes my hand *good thing we're in love,*
then, isn't it //

Window

Jordyn does it all the time how bad can it be
but I'm going to rip her dress

even so like where was she when I wanted
to leave drags me to the party & disappears

probably drunk already so is it oak tree
which let's be fair I do not have Jordyn's

arms or doorbell why didn't I bring a key
what kind of child leaves her own house & doesn't bring

a key but Nick hoists me onto the first branch & thank
you, past Daisy, for leaving the window open a crack

somehow I do it, my strength more than I know
then quickly out of the dress—unripped, another

miracle—and into my Tweety Bird pajamas
I fold the dress & arrange the butterflies

under my green desk lamp lock the window
and crawl into bed

but I can't sleep, sky slowly empurpled
then breaking blue and for a moment I wonder

if it's the sky I'm looking at, or
the sea

Daddy

The English teacher gives us Sylvia Plath

Daddy, daddy, you bastard, I'm through

gives us the whole story, the poet husband,

her head in the oven

somehow she makes the tragedy sizzle // the poems get deep in my bones

but that's her particular beauty, just a few years out of school

young & smart & pretty I try to imagine her life,

maybe a one-room apartment filled with books maybe

she brings men back or maybe she lets no one in

what does she eat for breakfast, a cup of black coffee Special K

when my father picks me up at school I'm abuzz but he looks past me

& I see his eyes run over her as if he's picking out a tie

Knocking

My father's fist against the door, the door
open, Jordyn & my father in the door

where did you go I was worried sick! & *Daisy*
what's all this about a party & *you told my father*

& *of course I told your father we couldn't find you*
anywhere we were out all night & *what is this*

about all night, Margaret Faye? & *is that makeup?*
My mother in the doorway now & my whole skin

glittering from Jordyn's lotion, my skin glittering
like a butterfly's wings *Daisy you left without telling me*

Well I couldn't find you could I & *Girls, girls* &
Jordyn thank you for your concern, why don't you

head home so we can talk to Daisy?
Her eyes on me are the eyes

of a snake *make sure she tells you the truth* she says, that last piece
just to be wicked, telling me she could ruin me & I'd better be careful.

But she knows me so well—of course
I was going to say she & Gretchen dragged

me to a party. Doesn't matter anyway
because when she leaves all I can get

out is *Nick invited us, Mama* & *well that's just*
the thing, isn't it, after we opened our home & wallets

to him, just the thing to invite our child
to participate in college debauchery &

yes, child, this is something I can work with
I'm sorry Mama I'm sorry Daddy

Nick invited us and Jordyn wanted to go
nothing happened I swear I didn't touch

the drinks or the food I walked in, said
hello to Nick, used the ladies' room,

realized my mistake and asked Nick
to drive me home. They're softening,

I can see it, like butter left out
for brunch *but, pumpkin, how did you*

get in why didn't you wake us? Think fast
Daisy *I brought a key with me* I shrug *the extra*

key, I put it back in the dish on the front hall table
don't know why I thought to do it but I had a key

They're nodding now, this is over though
who knows what else is over? & what

do I mean when I say I realized
my mistake? *Well that's good, pumpkin*

that's very responsible to bring a key
I smile, I have the nail for the coffin

well Daddy I thought what if I came home
while you and Mama were sleeping?

Though who knows if he was home
last night at all *good thinking. What say*

we ask Patty to fix us some breakfast
what would you like, muffin? French toast?

I'm nodding cartoonishly like the bird
on my pajamas *the very thing, Daddy*.

Chair

All week it's awkward at school Jordyn insisting there's nothing to talk about
so Friday afternoon I borrow Mama's car drive east
of East Egg to the mall park & make my way
to the Icing because I need something to break down whatever has grown
up between us. Try on a few necklaces that come together at the apex
of my clavicle then dangle down forming a Y & *why* I still couldn't
say why I left the party not because it was a mistake surely
but something in that exchange with Glasses Girl made me feel
the child I am at the Nelson School I found a necklace
like this one, the clasp had broken
and a girl had lost it & when Jay found who it was & gave it back
she looked at him for just a moment like he was nothing, like he'd stolen it
before her face broke into a smile *Gatsby*, his last name, which everyone
else called him both because that's what boys did & because
he was somehow of the staff & not of them, handsome though & she looked
at his tanned wrists & crossed her legs her Adidas
with iridescent stripes the same baby blue as Jordyn's dress that cool
blue for cool girls *Can I help you, miss*? & all apologies I take off
the necklace because I'm not here for me
& anyway that's too much of a gift for Jordyn that's an I-secretly-love-you gift
not a please-continue-to-love-me gift wander out and past
a kiosk selling beanie babies wonder for a moment if that would be cute
but the idea makes me feel like a child head into Claire's & pick
out the inflatable chair I know she's coveting, something
to make her childhood bedroom feel more like a dorm next year, even though
she's pretty much living at Gretchen's co-op already & for a minute I think
about them breaking up, not because I want them to break up
but because it feels good sometimes to think about broken things,
like a hummingbird that flew into the dining hall

and then knocked the window trying to get out & Jay picked it up
& cradled it in his hand,
the ruby chest rising and falling, rising & falling &
we took it outside & sat so quiet beneath the big tree its low branches
Jay I called him, though everyone else called him Gatsby, his name a bird flying
upside-down in my mouth *Daisy* and we sat like that with just our names
        between us
& waited until the bird regained its strength it came to with a sudden intensity
it couldn't wait to get away from us & this is more embarrassing
than the beanie babies but I cried to see it fly
it was such a small thing I couldn't imagine it just staying broken
Just the chair? & I add a notebook under lock & key
with a purple stuffed-animal cover because I'm almost out of pages in this one

Liquidate

Debt is leverage.

It's always been Tom & me against the world, our connection electric, but
        was it ever meant
          to last? Wasn't it meant to be first love, a disposable camera
of kissing photos, a song I can never hear without thinking
          of you?

          What our fathers built together should belong to us separately
          but it only belongs to Tom if we're together.

Chickens

All week when I've called Jordyn
her mother says *Oh Daisy, I'm sorry,*

she's at Gretchen's though who really knows
so today I just drive over & ring the doorbell,

the inflatable chair folded in a package in my arms,
and when a tall boy answers he calls for Gretchen.

She's surprised to see me insofar as she wasn't expecting me
but the look on her face says she's not surprised, really

Jordyn's at school late, she joined yearbook
because she was behind one elective credit. Not knowing this detail

makes me feel like I don't know Jordyn at all, like she isn't
even mine. *Come in anyway*, Gretchen says, ushering me

into the messy kitchen, a bowl of onions and potatoes
on the cracked counter. *Tea?* As she puts the kettle on

I see the stark truth: I am a child & she chooses chamomile
without asking me what I'd like & I can see what Jordyn sees

in her. *Things still a bit tangled between you & Jordyn?* she asks.
Outside the window chickens peck their evening seed.

I really did look for you I say but it comes out empty
& immature. *Oh I'm sure*, Gretchen gestures

over her shoulder & out the window, *it's just*
we chickies have to stick together. Foxes & all that.

The Phone Call

I'm working on my applications upstairs, lights
off except for the banker's lamp

to give things a feeling of beginning.
Phone rings, lighting up

the translucent case on my desk, startling me.
Father answers, his mumbled voice

through the floorboards, his feet
on the stairs, a knock at my door,

it's for you, pumpkin & he pads back
downstairs. I pick up, *hello?*

The sound of an AOL dialup connection
faint in the background, then my father

picking up the kitchen phone again, his breathing.
Daisy? It's me, Nick. I'm . . . calling to apologize.

I should never have invited you to that party
(my father sets the receiver back in its cradle)

Sorry Nick (hushed tones) *I had to say something*
I know you didn't invite us thank you

for driving me home & he loosens up
a little *yeah it's OK hey listen*

I'm at the library but I have something to give you
my neighbor was really sorry he missed you

He's not making any sense *your neighbor?*
Awkward laugh from Nick *yeah you know*

what's funny I think he likes hosting the parties
more than the parties themselves I never really

see him on the dance floor or drinking or anything
but he wanted me to give you something

Why me? He doesn't know me I'm a high school girl.
Couldn't tell you Daisy but I promised

when can I see you?

Chickens (II)

New chicks at the barn
so delicate you'd wonder

why the mother hens
trusted us with them

at all but Jay was so gentle
scooping one up & holding

it against my cheek, its honeyed
feathers. We went back

to his room after, his room
under the dining hall, &

he held me that same way,
like something he had to be careful with

& care for, soft as a feather but delicate
as bones you could break in your hand

Date Night

It rained during the movie
and the asphalt is wet

& glowing. I slap
the hood of Tom's car

why don't you ever let me drive?
He bats my hand away *hey*

gentle with her, yeah & when I laugh
& bat for the car again

he takes my shoulders & pushes me
against the passenger side door

then presses his body up against me
& kisses me the way you kiss

the woman you love, the woman
you plan to marry. Yellow lights

reflect & multiply on the wet ground.
I wrap my arms around his waist

& pull him into me. He's hard
everywhere. Run my hands

over his gelled hair, feel the iced tips
abrasive against my skin.

My silk slippers are getting wet
from the ground & I don't care.

Tom. His mouth like popcorn
and Junior Mints. *I'd better*

take you home runs his hands up
& down my sides *I can't wait*

for prom I've got my index
fingers in the belt loops

of his JNCOs pulling him
into me can't tell

if I want him or just love
to feel this wanted

Easy girl he says after a while
pulling away then *hey I left*

my jacket inside he unlocks the car
I'll be right back & he's off

through the cold parking lot leaving
me alone in the dark I hurry

into the car, pull a T-shirt over my tank top
so Mama doesn't know I went out

in spaghetti straps. Finger the key
in my purse, a reminder

that Mama and Daddy don't wait up
when I'm out with Tom. I uncap

my strawberry Lip Smacker & rub
it on my chapped lips. Maybe

Tom will want to mess around
a little more before he takes me

home. In the sun visor mirror,
I see a girl awake in her body.

Daisy, they call me, & I am
a flower springing

from the wet earth. I bite
my own strawberry lips.

When I flip the visor up
Tom is standing outside

the movie theater talking
to someone. He still doesn't

have his jacket. A girl, it looks
like, though I can't see her face,

wearing a white tee under a sundress
dappled in sunflowers despite

the chilly weather. Still can't see
her face. Tom gestures toward

the car. I can't be sure but it looks like
she touches his arm, the arm facing away

from me. He nods and heads back to the car,
opens the door, slides in, kisses me

on the cheek. *No luck?* I ask *No* he says
you know I could've sworn I brought my jacket

in rummages in the backseat *oh, duh, I left*
it in the car my brow furrows *funny you didn't*

check here first he kisses me again, lips this time,
distractedly *yup good thing I'm a Brown legacy,*

right Daze? Not the brightest crayon in the box
now am I? I touch his arm, *my* arm

now you know that's not what I meant.
Who were you talking to? He shrugs

just asking someone if she'd seen my jacket
as the car loops around the parking lot

I catch sight of the sunflowers and crane
my neck, just catching a glimpse

of her unforgettable glasses.

Swim Hole

On the last Sunday of the Nelson School, Jay takes me to a swim hole

parking his dad's jalopy under a canopy of fir trees

he jumps in from the bridge, swears

it's deep enough, but I'm too chicken

and I make my way down & around

on the slick rocks, slipping

only once.

Jay kisses my ankle, tells me the fresh water

has healing properties & pulls

me in before I have time to strip down

to my underwear. Afterward he smokes a clove cigarette

with his legs still dangling in the water.

I go home tomorrow, I remind him, like he needs reminding *I know,*

he says,

I was thinking I could visit over fall break

& his words hit me like a sun-warmed stone I have not

mentioned Tom

once all summer

Heart

Monday Jordyn brings a peace offering,
a friendship necklace, a heart

split in two. *So you know I love you forever,*
even when we fight, she tells me, her canvas

jacket rough over the blue dress I gave
back, into which she changed

in the girls' room, an olive branch.
Which do you want, she asks, *best or friends*

and I say *best* without thinking. She affixes
the necklace struggling

with the lobster clasp *you didn't tell me*
about yearbook I say & her face

falls *what I really didn't tell you*
is that Gretchen & I broke up

Seniors have open campus
so we're sitting on the back fields

ditching AP French. *What?*
You guys seemed so happy. What

gives? Jordyn wipes her nose
on her army surplus sleeve

I'm too young for her, somehow
she says, her voice cracking

only two years younger I say
yes but she decided it was holding

her back to date someone still in high
school, what does that even mean,

holding her back? I grab Jordyn
in a hug & press her body

into mine while she looks
over my shoulder *what*

can I do? I ask. Jordyn pulls
back. *Come with me tonight*
back to the party house,

she says & I realize
our conversation

was always headed here,
that the necklace with its words

was always a gift that demanded
something in return.

Please, Daisy. Gretchen won't even talk
to me anymore because she says

we both need to move on but I know
she's going to be at that party.

Please, Daisy. I shrug & adjust
my best *even if I said yes,*

I tell her, *we'd never get away with it*
again. There's no way my parents

are going to let me sleep over.
She pushes her curls

behind her ears, going in
for the kill. *We'll find*

a way. Daisy, please.
You owe me.

Love (II)

Was it Jay   himself
or the thrill of   something new?
was it love or lust   or just a craving
for freedom? Hope   or hope's shadow?
Do I love him still   or do I just feel
spoiled, now, for   Tom? Am I im-
pure or was I never pure to be-
gin with or was I the purest
version of myself with
Jay I thought only
of myself or is
that just
an   (other cliché)

Mix

Nick's waiting by the car
after school like I expected.
Mama let me take it & use the senior lot for once
though I didn't tell her why. *Hey* I say & *hey* he says,
because we have to say something.
Hands me a cassette tape, no case. *What the hell*
do you think he means by this he shrugs *listen I don't get it either*.
Then why help? Why make the drive?
Let's just say I owe him a favor, Nick explains.

Creep

The first song on the mix is "Creep" by TLC, so, like, OK,
at least Nick's neighbor has a sense of humor, although

this might be what Jordyn would call *too meta*, run a stop
sign as I wonder why the mix opens with a song

about a cheating boyfriend, my mind flashing
to Glasses Girl outside the movie

theater, the way her arm bent at an odd angle
as she touched him, or didn't. Slam

on the brakes at a light, take a deep breath.
Either she touched him, or she didn't & anyway

it's projection, right? Classic projection,
as Jordyn would say, quoting her mother.

That's all it is, Daisy. Keep it together.
I take a deep breath. Maybe something

happened at one of the house parties
when Tom went without me and without

telling me but even if it did, how would Nick's
neighbor know he has a girlfriend, why

would some stranger care? & anyway Tom's
never said anything to make me doubt myself,

keeps calling our prom night plans
visiting Providence, reminding me he means

forever, reminding me he means business.
Much more likely Nick's neighbor caught

a glimpse of me, maybe that Sunday
after brunch, & has developed a crush.

It's happened before. I have that
je ne sais quoi that boys like,

arms that look good springing
glitter-glanced from thin straps

or tight sleeves. & likelier still
I'm projecting my guilt onto Tom—

after all, I'm the one who cheated.
That summer I gave everything

to Jay including what I can't get back.
You'll tell him it happened horseback riding

and I will, I'll take it to the grave,
my grave beside his grave,

Tom's I mean. The tape clicks
over to the next song, Green

Day, "When I Come Around." Yes.
This makes sense. This stands

to reason. I am coming around
to common sense I am coming

around to my sharper faculties
I will come on prom night

& tell Tom it's the first time
all around. This is just a crush

tape. *Creep*—I'm crushing
on you. *When I Come Around*

we'll meet, because I only
caught a glimpse of you last

time through the dirty
bay windows. Do I need

to listen to any more? Well
maybe just until I get home.

I steer the hull of my mother's
old station wagon back

toward our street. This is fine.
This is more of the same and everything

is going according to plan.

Nights

I'm almost home when the song changes & from static
the opening strains of a familiar song congeal

my stomach in my throat I pull over by the playground & put the car in park

children run, children shout
silent through the window crows
scatter then land back together why

won't my hands stop shaking

It's the Smashing Pumpkins' "*Tonight, Tonight*," orchestral & cruel &
Jay

used to play this song in his car
the winding roads of Vermont ahead of us

all dark futurity
then suddenly lights through the windshield refracting like a star sapphire

his hand on my leg my eyes everywhere but on his face
his face so beautiful it hurt to look at, sometimes

strong scarred arms, bad haircut, smile that could explode the world
Jay the song is right I'm not the same & I realize this is not a crush, I

have been a fool, this is blackmail

this is someone who knows everything & will get what he wants
because I will give it I will give anything to protect myself, to protect Tom
I mean, I will do anything to make things stay

the same, I will never be the same, I will never feel that way again

Daddy (II)

He would give me anything would give me the world & if I had been a boy
he would have given me the company

orange juice on Christmas morning, *pour me a scotch, pumpkin*
& when I told him what I knew he didn't explain

just said *let's just say old Buchanan had it coming*
& I'll always provide for you and Tom, you know that

The starch of his shirts, the starch of his smile, arch.
His absence.

Window (II)

Can't tell Jordyn can't tell anyone
Grow up Daisy only you can fix this

Jordyn has her own problems
Jordyn knows all your secrets to boot

her *you owe me* wasn't not a threat can't spread this further
need to fix this & I realized

as I pulled into the garage maybe
it was Nick all along *opened our homes*

to him opened our wallets to him can't explain
how he knows but he knows

and the only thing I can think of really
side-eye Jordyn spraying Love's

Baby Soft on her freckled clavicle
is that he got it out of her, got her

drunk, or when she was mad at me,
or fresh from her breakup with Gretchen,

frankly I can see her & Nick naked
in the bed of their betrayal *never*

tell Daisy I told you this but
Shake my head, no time

for this, it isn't helping.
Lock my door & put a soothing

nature sounds CD in the boom
box, hope my parents assume

I'm sleeping & can't hear them.
Key on a piece of mother's yarn

tucked deep into my shirt, secure
beneath my bra strap. I'm dressed

more like Glasses Girl this time,
like I don't care, and I don't.

Dark brown lipstick with no
other makeup, plaid shirt

I borrowed from Tom,
my favorite Express jeans,

perfectly broken in, tube
socks, white Keds. I look

like I don't give a damn.
I look hot though let's

be real. What could Nick want?
Money, probably. Thought

the whole family was wealthy
but haven't we learned

it’s time for me to grow up
& learn something about

the world? Maybe Jordyn’s
in on it, know she needs money.

How do I look? Crushed velvet
& a crushed smile, I’m crushed

with guilt for a minute but still
not convinced. *Beautiful you know*

you look beautiful. Reach over,
unclasp her *friend* necklace, lay

it on my desk beneath the green
light, pull a black velvet choker

out of the drawer, lean over and clasp
it around her delicate neck. ~~For a moment~~

~~I want to kiss her if only from the nerves~~
~~& desperation.~~ We swing out the window

as if the night is ours, leaving
the light on.

Liquidate (II)

As a child I loved that book, *If You Give a Mouse a Cookie*.

He'll want milk next, and then he'll eat you alive.

Debt is leverage.

If Tom finds out I cheated, it will crush his fragile pride.

I'll be one more person who was supposed to love him, but didn't.

If I crush his fragile pride, he's going to want a tall glass of breaking up with me.

If he breaks up with me, and I inherit the company, then somebody else will
have to run it.

Whoever I marry will have to run it.

Jay or the next one, or the one after that, or the one after that, while Tom's cut out of a fortune that should have been his, cut out and chopped up and sold for parts, sold for parts just like the heart it takes so much for him to give, that warm heart beating all alone in that big cold house.

The Party

"Big Poppa" is playing but where is that drip of a cousin?
I push in the doors & look everywhere for him

no sign & even if I saw the host I wouldn't recognize him.
Jordyn grabs my hand. *There she is.*

Go, I say, trying to sound the way a supportive friend would sound,
trying to be a supportive friend. *Go to her* & a gentle push on the small

of her back. Jordyn stumbles to Gretchen, a vision in velvet, Gretchen
catches sight of her, doesn't break off

her conversation. *Nick.* He's not dancing, not in the kitchen,
        not in the hallway,
not in the bathroom, not in the formal dining room

that's been converted to a pothead's paradise, trippy posters
& beanbag chairs, not on the back steps where a couple

is tangled up together. I head upstairs because what else can I do
but there's nobody up here, nobody at all. Sneak out the back door,

muttering apologies as I navigate around the couple.
Thought they were making out but they seem engrossed

in conversation. Gotta get to Nick's dorm, find Nick,
confront Nick & get back to the party

before Jordyn notices I ditched her again.
For a moment in the alley I realize how vulnerable

I am, remember Mama's
warnings, but there's no time for that now.

Easy to slip into the dorm dressed, as I am,
like a college girl, & there are names on the doors

so I look for *Nick C.* Can't explain why
but I take the key off my neck before I knock,

wedge it between my fingers, because what
if I need to hit him? Stranger things have happened.

Lift my fist, small but sure, & knock.

Alone

Alone together in Tom's house after school, fall of freshman year.

/ / /

Family photographs glared down on us.

/ / /

He turned on *MTV* & I kissed the back of his neck,

quivering skin like a cliff jump

Smoke

Nick opens the door in a cloud of smoke, the room thick
with the fleshy smell of marijuana. *Phew, Daisy.* He exhales.

Thought you were my RA again & I'd lose this for sure. Lifts a pill
jar full of small, green buds, gray through the orange

plastic. This is not the greeting of someone blackmailing me.
This is the greeting of my boring cousin, stoned

& oblivious. Another boy behind him barely visible in the smoke—
his roommate, or a friend? I cut

to the chase. *What was with that mixtape anyway?*
Nick shrugs & the shrug, I see, is genuine.

Ask my neighbor. I don't even know what's on it.
I gesture behind me, back toward the party, though

I'm turned around from the riot-proof dorm halls
and couldn't tell you which way the house is

*I was just at his party, I don't even know which one
he is.* Nick laughs a little too enthusiastically.

Why don't you come in for a minute?

~~Ocean~~

~~When you sneak out the window you go~~
~~down~~

~~into the depths of something, the sky~~
~~is ocean-blue, the depths~~

~~of a room you enter, a room~~
~~filled with smoke~~

~~[something about emotion, here? memory]~~

Do I hate this poem? Please circle one:

Yes No Maybe

Remix

Grateful Dead posters, lava lamp, some random jam blasting
a typical dorm for a typical dude.

I've got my arms crossed tight against my chest
as if to protect me from the smoke, as if that's even

possible. There's a guy facing away from me in a swivel
desk chair, holding a bong but not smoking, holding a pipe like a pipe. I feel

the smoke get to me a little bit,
a tingle down my spine.

Jay turns around to face me.

Do you want to get out of here?

Alley

How are you here? Tears slide
down my cheeks, standing
in the alley between the dorm

and his house, "Electric Slide" muffled
by the walls, its volume intensifying

every time the door opens.

Every time the door opens, we lower our voices.
What was this whole thing, some trap?

Jay's eyes are on fire. I am on fire. I am made of fire,
myself am fire.

You could call it a trap, Daze.
I'd call it a gesture.

Which part is a gesture?

Moving here this summer, the parties, the whole thing, Daisy.

Your whole life is a gesture?

He catches my hands, pulls me toward him. I straighten my arms
to assert distance but I'm melting, I'm falling

to pieces, I'm falling apart.

You're the love of my life, Daisy.
Of course my whole life's a gesture.

I'm about to sink into him—*my soul began*

its first sink into her,
deep, heady, lost; like drowning

in a witches' brew,
but I can't. I peel

my arms away. *Jay I have a boyfriend.*
A wrinkle creases his brow

as it dawns on him, this thing
I have never said out loud.

Did you always have a boyfriend?

Jay.

Answer the question, Daisy.
Did you always have a boyfriend?
Is that why you disappeared

after the summer, is that why you didn't want me
to come for fall break?

I'm disappearing now, I think,
a flower exposed to frost

and shivering, a flower that would have fed
on the water of those memories

for a lifetime & finds by her own poison

the source drying up

Jay

The truth this time

It's not like that

What is it like, Daisy?

I don't have to tell you, Jay, because we were together

two summers ago and it's

spring of senior year I'm applying

for college I'm going away

with Tom we're going to get married

Married? Daisy you're eighteen

Don't care and anyway we won't marry right away

we have a plan Tom has a plan you can't bring the past

here you can't touch our future can't trick me can't

have me back

He's blasted, I see it, his face

a broken hope *Daisy,*

first love is worth fighting for, Daisy

You were my first, I spit back, *but not my last*

a lie and I know it & maybe

I am a witch, maybe I conjured him with my guilt & lust
& bad poems am I haunted

by what happened that summer? The moon as red as the blood
that stained the blanket.

Steps

I am sinking
in the water, I am

coming up for air

Jay loves me Jay would never hurt me
never tell Tom and so what if he does

I'll say he's lying what will Tom do?
Believe some stranger over me?

As I walk away from him in the alley I feel
myself vulnerable to the dark, I feel myself

press through the haunting & there are the back steps,
there's the couple no, a different couple now, their bodies

entangled, the passion rising off them like infrared light.
Of course after all this I have to interrupt them,

hot & heavy like a *Cosmo* how-to, biting
each other's lips in the almost-dark,

but I have to come in the back way
can't risk Jordyn knowing I left

Jordyn, who's probably crying
in the bathroom by now.

Jay's house. This is Jay's house.
A house where he throws parties

even though as I recall he hates to party
finds them *lonely* a crowd like that is *lonely*

if you want to go skinny-dipping at the duck pond
with everybody I'll come with you but I'd rather stay

here with you, Daisy, with the moonlight
through the window as I get closer to the stairs my eyes adjust

his hands on her in her black tank top
her round-brushed hair like a starlet's

tangling in his hands *sorry* I think before
I can say it *sorry to interrupt the stuff of life*

so I can sneak into this sham of a party
& pretend to be a good friend! But instead I clear

my throat & they take their mouths
off each other & the girl looks at me, squints

really, her face coming into focus, squints
and unhooks her glasses from her bra,

her familiar face clicks into place
as she sets her glasses on her nose

tortoiseshell, her grandfather's, coming
down to her from the fullness of time

and blessing her beauty. *Hey*, she says,
as if we've known each other forever,

and maybe we have. *I'm so sorry*, I say.
I'm sorry, too, she says, & wipes

her lip gloss off my boyfriend's face.

Run

Daisy, Tom says, but before he can reach me
I've run past him into the house

& you know Tom would never make a scene
I'm the one who's crying

Jordyn's eating chips & guacamole in the kitchen
with Gretchen and another girl

I come in looking destroyed, Jay & Tom
both ruined in the same night,

I am a spilled beer, I am a beer spilled and running
off the counter & drying on the floor sticky

staying sticky *Jordyn I have to go Jordyn where's the car*
& Gretchen has my shoulders *hold on a second*

you're not going anywhere & she's right,
it's not like Tom's coming after me, not now anyway.

You're both coming back to the co-op with me she says, decisive, sober,
walking us back to the car & piloting it down the cobbled

streets of West Egg more competently than I could have done.
Tucks us in with throw pillows

on a sofa thrice-handed-down, heats up some vegan soup.
Are you guys back together at least? I ask Jordyn when she's in the kitchen.

We're going to take a step back & be friends for now
but I feel better, Jordyn tells me, winks. *She might*

come to prom with me as friends, how badass would
that be? A fresh stream of tears springs

down my cheeks and she moves over to me, wraps
her arms around my quaking shoulders & it all

comes out, Glasses Girl, the Smashing Pumpkins,
the alley, Jay, all of it

I tell her everything because someone has to know me
& it might as well be her, my fingers fiddling

with the *best* on my necklace. I'm not the best at anything
but Jordyn is the best I've got.

Just a Girl (II)

I let myself in with the key this time,

    not a girl anymore and who cares   if they hear me?

Key in the lock

        its click the only thing   I'm sure of.

Of course they don't hear me.

Of course they don't care.

        My father probably isn't even home.

I drop the key in the dish,   take the stairs slowly

    & knock on my parents' bedroom door.

Daddy (III)

He'd give me the world but then I see

him take in the waitress, her curves

filling his eyes, her image running

down his face like egg yolk.

What would he think

if somebody looked at me

that way?

Pedestal

Mama's there alone, as I suspected, her face haggard without makeup, pink
dressing gown. Can't tell her about Jay, obviously, can't

tell her about Nick, the tape, the Nelson School but my face
crumples into tears and she pulls me to her bed

her touch unexpected on my arm. Finally I get my voice.
Mama I went to a party with Jordyn I'm sorry I didn't want to go

Gretchen broke up with her and she needed me, Mama.
Mama, Tom was there . . . Tom was there kissing another girl.

I raise my eyes, ashamed, to meet her gaze.
I'm surprised to find her unsurprised. *Mama?*

She looks at me the way she did the first time
I menstruated, like I am complaining about an inevitable

inconvenience. *Mama he was . . . making out with her. Another*
girl. A college girl, I think. On the . . . back steps of the house.

My mother blinks thoughtfully, clears her throat.
What were you doing behind a house at night? Party

or no party, you're leaving for Providence this summer
& I can't protect you forever, what could you mean

outside the house at night? Didn't I tell you
about girls who walk alone at night?

I shake my head in disbelief *Mama.*
Tom, Mama. She pulls a cigarette out

of her nightstand, lights it, takes
a long drag, exhales. I didn't know

she smoked. *Yes, pity, that. Bound*
to happen sooner or later. Maybe

waiting until after graduation to marry
isn't the best idea. As long as he's got

you on a pedestal, well now. It's a quote
from a romantic comedy—me

on a pedestal & Glasses Girl in his arms—
even at a moment like this,

my mother can only repeat sound bites.
You'd marry him anyway? I ask—insensitive,

in retrospect, considering my father is nowhere
to be seen—and she laughs, a hard laugh

deep in her throat like a swallowed lozenge.
Now, we've spoiled you even more than I thought.

That face, that money, that family, and you
expect chastity, too? All men stray. She takes me

in from tip to tail. *Must be something*
he's not getting at home, yes? She's drunk,

I realize, taking in the tumbler empty
on the dresser, the open canister

of pills. *Good night, Mama.* Back in my room
I lock the door, call Tom's house, hang up

before it rings.

Stitch

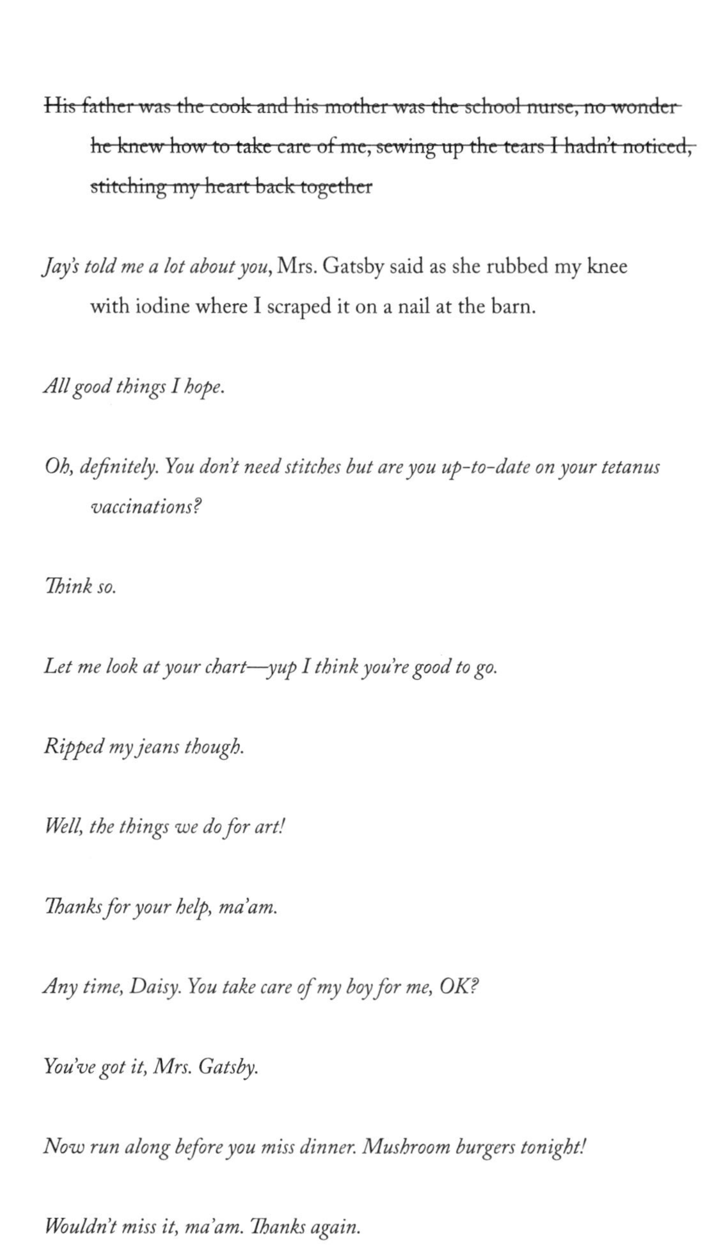

~~His father was the cook and his mother was the school nurse, no wonder he knew how to take care of me, sewing up the tears I hadn't noticed, stitching my heart back together~~

Jay's told me a lot about you, Mrs. Gatsby said as she rubbed my knee with iodine where I scraped it on a nail at the barn.

All good things I hope.

Oh, definitely. You don't need stitches but are you up-to-date on your tetanus vaccinations?

Think so.

Let me look at your chart—yup I think you're good to go.

Ripped my jeans though.

Well, the things we do for art!

Thanks for your help, ma'am.

Any time, Daisy. You take care of my boy for me, OK?

You've got it, Mrs. Gatsby.

Now run along before you miss dinner. Mushroom burgers tonight!

Wouldn't miss it, ma'am. Thanks again.

Take care of my boy, the type of thing people often say but rarely
mean, but she meant it. Jay, sensitive as a seismometer, running
his fingers over my skin, registering the earthquakes underneath,
my skin quaking,
my breath quaking, my whole body
like soil wet from the rain
my whole self sporing, sprouting forth
like those mushrooms that spring up after the rain and, just as suddenly,
are gone

Progress

Nick's over, for dinner this time, and he's brought some boring girl with even less to say than he has.

A creative writing major? she says. *That sounds fun.*

Yup it'll be a real picnic.

Daisy, please be a good host.

How are your applications going, by the way?

Thanks for asking, Nick. They're going swimmingly if by swimming you mean drowning.

Oh, that was quite funny! I can tell you're a writer. Nick, you didn't tell me your cousin was so funny.

Now, speaking of applications, Nick, have you given any thought to summer internships? My investment firm's hiring an intern, as a matter of fact. Unpaid, of course, but you can't beat the experience.

Darling, let Nick make his own way. You were young too, once.

Thanks for the tip. Haven't given much thought to the summer yet, but I'll think about that. How are things at the firm these days?

Good, but busy. Lots of long nights in the city.

Redundancy

Another boring poem with no epiphany
for you, Jay. For you, Tom.

For you, Nick. For you, Daddy.
Another boring poem rife

with disappointment. Used to think
of my poems as the place where I could

go deep ~~but now I realize there's nothing~~
~~deep about me but here I am in the depths~~

~~of despair but I'm in too deep~~

They call me the submarine girl
I go down but nothing touches me

Return

Borrow Mama's car, park it crooked in the alley
& bang on the back door because I have come
from the past to claim what is rightfully mine.

Jay opens it, first the door and then the screen,
the shock of him here, not just in West Egg
but in the present. *What do you want, Daisy?*

A thousand lies flicker over my skin
but in the end I tell him the truth.
I'm applying to college & I thought

my poetry was getting better but now you
showed up & the past doesn't feel nostalgic
anymore and Tom kissed another girl

so the future doesn't feel nostalgic
either and I'm so mad at you for showing
up & butting in on my life like I'm yours

to take like we can pick up where we left off
like I'm a butterfly under glass I don't want
you anymore but I need something

for my poetry I need material his eyes
shoot sparks *you don't love me anymore*
you just want to use me for your poetry

and mad as it sounds coming
from his practical mouth
that's exactly what I mean

so I nod, my chin making the point
& he lets out all the air in his lungs
more air than makes sense he sounds

like a horse after being run too long. He shrugs
his shoulders. *I can live with that.*

Tom

Tom apologizes with flowers & a silver ring
shaped like a daisy, a pearl at its center.

My promise to you, he says. *My promise*
that I'm yours, that the engagement

and wedding and marriage you expect
are coming—and I can't wait. Daze,

I can't wait, I was drunk, I was thinking
of you the whole time, Daisy, I'm sorry,

Margaret Faye, will you forgive me?
Will you marry me someday?

Slide that daisy on my finger
& kiss him more tenderly

than he deserves but then,
I've had a lot of practice lately.

Course I forgive you ya big dummy
& he groans into my mouth

I cannot wait for prom, Daisy.
I push him back just slightly,

playfully. I am a girl on TV
showing my belly button

beneath a cut-off T-shirt,

I am a princess greeting my subjects.

Well now who says I'm going with you?

Isn't there anyone else you'd like to ask?

His lips on my collarbone

right here in the burger joint

Daisy don't torture me I said I was sorry.

Still have to ask me.

And you'll say yes?

Ask and you'll see.

Daisy. His hand on my knee under the table

but too hard this time, creeping

up my thigh

Yes I blurt out *yes Tom I'll say yes yes*

Yearbook

Jay picks me up most days after school now.
Told Mama I joined yearbook for a missing

credit. I write my applications at his house,
all five of them, carving a portfolio

out of the past and the present.
My personal statement reads

like a Smashing Pumpkins song.
We are young once, I say,

and we have the art of that youth,
art we hopefully carry with us

into age and wisdom, sure, but also art
that helps us experience our youth

before it's too late. What does it mean
to be a girl? I ask. What does it mean

to become a woman? How might the art
of my youth help me understand this time

in my life—both the art I make
& the literature I read, the music

I listen to? How does art help us
become who we are, and how might

it help us remember who we were?
What does it mean to experience

first love in relation to a particular
song? To hear that song again

with the wisdom we've gained
and feel changed but what if

the song is also about change—
about how you'll never be the same person

you are right now & maybe you aren't already?
Gretchen prints the statement at the co-op,

goes over it with a red pen. *Too meta*,
says Jordyn. They appear to be back

together but swear they aren't labeling things.
Jordyn got her early admissions acceptance

& wants to move into the co-op. Gretch
worries that they *each need their own space*,

Jordyn says *well living at home with my parents*
isn't exactly my own space, anyway, plays

with a leopard-print slap
bracelet, chasing Gretchen

around the room, flirtatious.
Jordy we need to focus need to get our girl into college!

I take all the mothering I can get, tell my mother
Tom & I will be out late for dinner

in the city with his grandparents & walk naked
around Jay Gatsby's dilapidated Victorian,

this mansion of our secrets that he bought—well, rented—
so that I would have room to be my imperfect self.

Torn

In class, I share a poem about poppies, red
against a blue sky, moved

by the wind but somehow plastic,
bending back, standing
tall

I call the petals flesh unzipped
I call them clothing on the floor

A hand reaches out

I call the sky the sea
I call the field the sea

A student raises
her hand, calls it *too Plathy*

the teacher winks
    at me
    as long as you're breathing, she says, *there's no such thing*

Polaroid

Jay takes a photo of us kissing
shakes it & I tell him *you're not supposed to shake it*

& he tells me *I'm waiting to see what develops*
& I say *what could develop*

& he says *don't start.* We mailed the applications
yesterday. *My girlfriend's applying to art schools,*

he told the postman. *And when are you gonna go*
to school, Jay? I teased him. *Can't wait tables*

forever he laughed, kissed me right there
holding up the line *you wait*

& see what I can do. But now the photo
is coming into focus & I do look

like his girlfriend, my hair a mess
and my arm thrown sloppily

around him. *She looked like his girlfriend*
I realize, remembering

how Glasses Girl wiped the gloss
from Tom's mouth & cheek. She apologized

to me, and not just for making out
on the stairs. She knew

who I was. She knew the first time.
I knew I recognized that plaid shirt

around her waist—it was Tom's.
Daisy, you OK? I don't know

if I'm OK. Does it make it worse
if it wasn't just a drunken mistake?

It doesn't make it better but maybe
it makes us even. I unbutton

the top button of my blouse.
I think we can take a better picture.

Semi-Charmed Life

Third Eye Blind concert in the field
house, a cacophony of bodies

jumping and singing
in the cavernous space despite

the bad acoustics. Paramedics
called to collect a dropped

crowd-surfer, Tom
buys a T-shirt & puts it on,

puts his arm around me.
Brought you here to ask you

something he yells in my ear
as we jump up & down

What

I said I need to ask you something

I can't hear you

Daisy

Break between songs, applause, his mouth
on my ear *Will you go to prom with me?*

I nod vigorously, jump
into his arms, jump

into our life together
all men stray I think *why*

not girls too & his hand
in the back pocket

of my jeans the tattoo
necklace marking my neck

as if drawing a line
between my head & my heart

after the concert, in the evening chill
steam rises off teenage bodies

I run back in to use the bathroom
lock eyes with Glasses Girl

on her way out in a pack of college friends
I expect venom but her eyes

give me sympathy
sympathy magnified

by her oversize lenses sympathy
that hurts worse than venom ever could

We Don't Talk about Tom

but today we have to because Jay's teasing me about prom.

We didn't have prom at the Nelson School, he tells me, *come on,*
it's cheesy but it'll be fun. Let me

put a corsage on your wrist—he kisses my wrist—*I just want to dance*

with my girl, I want the hokey posed pictures—he kisses my mouth—*I want*
everything
with you, Daisy.

I shake my head.

Why?

I just don't want to.

You don't want to go to prom?

I don't want to go to prom.

Bullshit, Daisy, of course you want
to go to prom want
the dress the flowers
I bet you're nominated for prom court, Daisy
You can lie to me Daisy
all you want but I'm not stupid

Fine I stand up and start to gather my things *I can't go to prom with you because I'm already going with Tom*

His face a blank image of disbelief *Tom?*

Tom? My boyfriend, Tom?

He stands up, grabs my wrist harder
than he's ever touched me

Your fucking boyfriend?
Are you fucking kidding me right now?

I never told you I broke up with him
you shouldn't make assumptions
you knew what you were getting yourself into we're squared

off in his living room shouting like a married couple

in this tired Victorian *the hell I did, Daisy*

told you I don't love you anymore

the hell you don't
maybe you didn't the day you came back but the hell
you don't, now

It doesn't matter anyway I'm going to prom with Tom

So you've been seeing us both this whole time

I thought you knew. You don't own

me I never said we were girlfriend-boyfriend
I literally said I was using you, Jay

You've been seeing us both this whole time? Yes or no

rage rises to the surface, burning
up his skin
a rage I might call love

Yes or no?

I nod I have nothing to say

Sleeping with us both?

I shake my head *no, Jay, I've never slept with Tom I've only slept with you.*

And that's when I see it.
That's when I see the dust settle.
I'm his, he thinks. He's won.

I've saved myself for him I'll save myself for him I won't marry anybody but him won't move away with anybody but him I belong with him I belong to him.

At that moment, I want to hurt him, so I do.

Tom and I have been waiting for prom night.

Sequins

No mom one without sequins, ugh! Jordyn & I are together
in a dressing room at Jessica McClintock,

our *best* and *friends* clanging against our chests,
our mothers outside making small talk

over to-go coffee, Jordyn's mom's topknot
& comfort with us both, with our bodies,

my mother looking at fabric swatches, *well*
you're a winter, dear, maybe bright blue?

How do you girls feel about asymmetrical hems
with fringe asks the overeager salesgirl,

& *just as friends still?* I ask, sliding into
a shiny black mermaid dress with pink

flaring stripes down the side. *With benefits,*
she winks. *Take that off. I've got you*

& she glides out into the store
in just her oversize sweater hanging

long over her underwear & comes back
with a slinky purple dress

overlaid in a blue mesh layer covered
with beaded flowers. *Daisies?* I laugh

& she mouths *because you're giving Tom*
your flower and we lose our shit

because the whole thing is just
too much, our mothers out there,

mine stilted & awkward in head-to-toe
Lilly Pulitzer & Jordy's in wild

pinned-up curls that match her daughter's mane
& a stretched-out sweater with oversize

buttons & we know this is a rite of passage
but Lord, have we passed beyond it me

juggling two men at once Jordyn longing
to move in with her college girlfriend

it's perfect, I say, while Jordyn settles
on a twirly skirt & corset top

to keep the girls in, she says,
her mother tucking in her bosom,

though these girls have let themselves out
& good luck tying us down

Slam

Jay's in the back corner of the coffee shop blasting
something on his Discman, headphones

protective against the ambient noise.
A barista is setting up a microphone,
clipboard balanced on a stool beside her

Jay has an untouched latte, a leaf
drawn in the foam & I

take a slow sip, the milk bubbles sticking
to my upper lip. Coffee makes me jittery

but who cares I'm jittery already.

What are you listening to? Jay fiddles with the buttons
Radiohead. The Bends. I nod *sounds depressing*

Not really he meets my eyes for the first time *thanks*
for meeting up to talk I tug

at my bra band my whole body feeling uncomfortable
my whole self feeling uncomfortable

in my body *yeah of course* I say *did you ask me here*
to break up with me

No, Daisy. I love you I'm not breaking up with you
asked you here to make you choose

Same thing I shrug *because I choose Tom*
    feedback from the microphone *Daisy*

Don't Daisy me I choose Tom
I'm going to prom with Tom I'm going to Providence with Tom

You got into RISD, then?

Not yet but I will

How do you know

Doesn't matter. Daddy made a donation
called someone he knows from growing up

Jay's eyes are skeptical
    What, you don't believe in me?

Of course I believe in you he gestures at the clipboard *put your name on the list*
  already
    Stop I wipe foam off my nose *I told you I don't do slam*
    my stuff is more visual, I like to play with the page

yeah you do he quips and I shake my head *come on,*
  give the people what they want

stop it

so you're just going to deny them?
        deny them or deny you? and we're back where we started

You'd really choose Tom?

I nod.

So you're breaking up with me then

Not breaking up with you just choosing you're
the one who made me choose

Fine I won't make you choose then

He can feel me slipping away & his eyes are on me & then his hand is on
my hand
on the table & his eyes are on my eyes are over my shoulder land
on Tom standing in the doorway

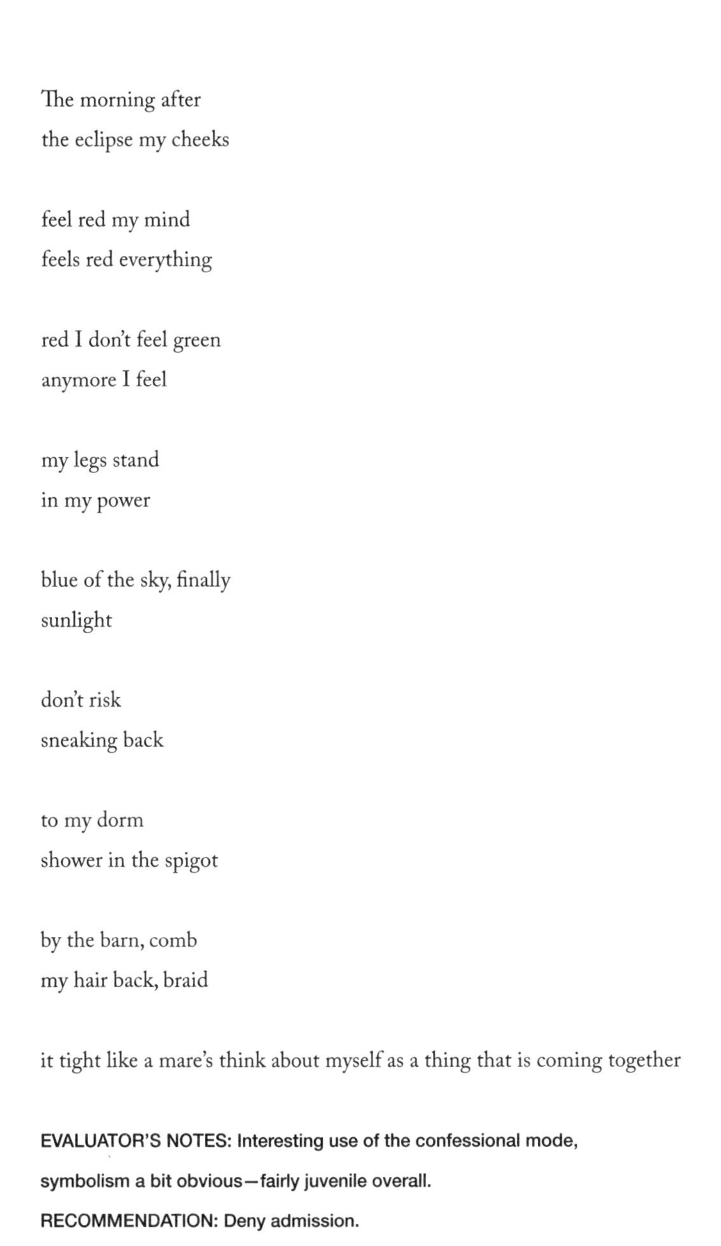

Power

The morning after
the eclipse my cheeks

feel red my mind
feels red everything

red I don't feel green
anymore I feel

my legs stand
in my power

blue of the sky, finally
sunlight

don't risk
sneaking back

to my dorm
shower in the spigot

by the barn, comb
my hair back, braid

it tight like a mare's think about myself as a thing that is coming together

EVALUATOR'S NOTES: Interesting use of the confessional mode,
symbolism a bit obvious—fairly juvenile overall.
RECOMMENDATION: Deny admission.

Rejections

Five small envelopes

like a chorus line

under the spotlight of a green banker's lamp

five direct missives (chorusing *no*)

Our daughter, the ~~writer~~ failure

Date Night (II)

Tom saw.
I know he saw.
Saw the blood drain from Jay's face & turned
my head just in time to see him
retreating through the coffee shop door

(the cruelty of the barista's smile, witnessing)

My first thought, odd I know, was *why*
does Jay recognize Tom has he been watching
me and the moment I thought it I knew

it must be so. Haven't talked to Tom
about it since & here we are sitting in the movie
theater no parts of us touching.

Does he know I saw him see?
After what happened

with Glasses Girl, better
to bring it up or not?

For all he knows it was nothing,
          for all I know I am nothing
at all. *Tom* I whisper and the couple

behind us goes *shhh* & Tom takes
my hand in his, my shaking hand,

runs his thumb across my knuckles.

Plans

The Sunday before prom I'm wearing chunky glitter heels around
the house in my pajamas with tube socks to break them in

Daisy, come in here we'd like to speak with you my parents at the kitchen
table, a place I so rarely see them alone together. I take my seat.

Daisy, we've been thinking about your future Daddy smiles & Mama
takes out a ring box, blue velvet. The diamond inside

is a glooming rectangle. *It was my grandmother's*, Daddy smiles.
Bite my lips, part my lips, close my mouth.

We know you're disappointed about RISD, pumpkin, but you can be
a writer even
without school

Try it on sweetie

Writing is a very respectable hobby

Plenty of writers never went to art school it's a liberal scam really

We think it best
We think We think it best Think it best dear We think it best pumpkin
Think it best Think it best you go Think it best you go to Providence
with Tom, muffin You know how those college girls can be Why
so very aggressive these days! And with those eyes and that money!
Such an eligible bachelor We think it best
We think it best dear Think it best pumpkin Why can you imagine

Tom Buchanan in a dormitory?   No that would never do we think it best
dear   Why
there are plenty of openings at the club this summer   something to take
your mind off RISD yes,   dear?   We think it best
the Buchanans think it best   and Tom
Tom dear
Why Tom is going to ask for our blessing, that's what the Buchanans said
why not start out in Providence in your own home, yes you're young   but you only
live once why waste time, dear   Now wouldn't that be nice pumpkin,
a summer wedding   on the water   why   back in our day
it was done all the time   We didn't need to sow our wild oats   like kids
these days   Jordyn's poor mother   Jordyn chasing after that, that hippy
when we all   know she'll settle down eventually   just try it on
we think it best dear we think it
best dear   Now muffin look at that just a little   too big
we'll have it sized,
dear   and then of course you'll fill out a bit, won't you   fat
and happy with   Tom in Providence   yes   don't think the plan's
off   because of those liberal farts
at RISD   just didn't see your brilliance   perhaps it's a blessing
in disguise after all   this gives you plenty of time to get your sea legs
before you think of children   in our day it was quite common
you're a special girl Daisy   with special gifts   to give
Margaret Faye Buchanan, have you ever   heard a lovelier name?

Oh yes this will be best

Plans (II)

Prom's in the city at a big hotel.
The school hired buses

but of course we're driving.
We're not kids anymore.

Tom's reserved a room
& I've picked out navy

blue lingerie to match
the mesh overlay

of my dress. In a way
I'm glad he's not my first,

not that he needs to know it.
Sounds like he'll be my last

after all. Providence, marriage.
After talking to my parents

I ran upstairs & called him.
What do you think I said

is this just coming from them
or is this what you're thinking too

he admitted it was his dad's suggestion
but why not, Daze? Gives you a plan

too, doesn't it & I had to admit
he had a point after all

what am I going to do, stay
home with Mama & Daddy?

It's too late to apply to other schools,
even state schools. Only thing

I can think of is a gap year, traveling
to Europe wandering museum

after museum in search of inspiration.
So let's do it Jay says we're sharing

a pizza sitting on the floor lifting
slice after slice right out of the box
after all it's time I *filled out a little*

break up with Tom and let's go abroad
Paris London Dubrovnik

What on your waiter's salary?

Listen I've got more saved than you realize.

How?

Daisy, where do I wait tables?

I search my brain & come up empty.
Not sure you've ever mentioned.

Daisy, I don't wait tables you think I could rent this house
& throw those parties on tips from college students?

I am even more naive than I thought. *What*
have you been doing for money then?

Let's just say that wasn't the first time Tom's seen me
& Nick would have found me if I hadn't found him first

You've been dealing pot?

Among other things. Not dealing other things. Just dealing pot and . . . tutoring.

The American Dream.

Don't know who you are to judge, exactly. You going to finish that slice?

No I think I've lost my appetite.

Listen Daisy I'm just helping people. Tutoring & dealing a little on the side.
Didn't tell you because I thought you didn't need to know about the dealing.
Serving
just serving up some tasty joints.

Fine I'm not one to judge you're right.

Listen it's not East Egg money but let me float the tickets,
we can do the hostel thing, live
on bread & cheese in France, you can write & maybe I'll go

to culinary school, take after my dad.
For a moment I think of saying yes,
weigh a wedding at the club against nights

spent writing at a café on the Left Bank. I'm a cliché,
I realize, in either direction. I'm a prize to be won.

My parents will disown me.

Don't mind Daisy I'm not in it for the money.

We'll go broke.

We can always stay at Nelson for a bit while we regroup.

I close my eyes for a moment
there on the hardwood floor

picture Paris
picture myself in a sundress by the river

a fountain pen behind my ear
then realize Jay is nowhere in the picture.

Don't plan a party in our room I tell Tom that night on the phone
the dance will be fun but I want to be alone with you as soon as possible.

~~Globe~~

~~The globe in my father's home office, the blue of its ocean, the places I could go~~
~~if I traveled after my finger, my finger landing on the planet, spun~~

~~He'd give me the world if he could, Tom too~~

~~would give me the world, would take it from me, from my~~
~~father~~

~~& who am I~~
~~to want something different?~~

~~*Your father knows best*, my mother's old refrain, the promise of Tom freed~~
~~from his family,~~
~~funded by mine~~

~~One look at my mother and I know my father's love is never~~
~~unconditional.~~
~~One look at Tom and I wonder at my own.~~
~~A million memories, a thousand promises.~~
~~I've just been messing around I've just been messing around I've just~~
~~been~~
~~messing around like the mess I am~~

The Last Night

Prom is Saturday so Friday night I'm staying in
writing & ~~doing some Bioré pore strips~~ purging myself of impurities.

Thursday night was the last night.
I didn't tell Jay but I told myself.

Made the night move in slow motion
kissed him in slow motion took control

made (myself) a memory.

After we went to the noodle place
~~fasted all day today so my tummy's still flat in my dress~~

~~noodles long like a life~~
~~noodles long like our lives apart~~
~~noodles stretching in different directions~~

steam from our bowls and clouds on our tongues.

Walking back we looked through curtainless windows in the dusk.
TVs on, students studying, practicing

instruments, laughter. One girl painting

in an upstairs bedroom, crystals hanging in her window
crystals that could reflect light, could make rainbows

but tonight there was only night her arms like dancers
red, blue, green across the canvas

She paused thoughtfully. She took a step back.
She looked at her creation and was satisfied.

Came to the window & gazed out at the stars
the stars reflecting off her grandfather's glasses.

Drive

You'd think we'd have a lot to talk about,
high school sweethearts driving to prom
on the precipice of engagement. Tom's
acceptance to Brown came yesterday—
turns out he was briefly waitlisted,
which he didn't bother to tell me, but now
he's in—and his father offered to buy
us a starter home in Providence
so long as Mama & Daddy pay
for the wedding. You'd think
we'd have a lot to talk about
but we're stuck in traffic & a silence
hangs in the air. Reach over & run
my hand down the front of Tom's body
& he smiles. *That's my girl.*

Save Tonight

Tom checks in & we check out the room
Tom's brought a canvas bag with pajama
pants, toothbrush, a bottle of vodka.

I didn't think to bring anything
besides my tiny beaded clutch
with lip gloss, driver's license,

& a condom Jordyn gave me
in case Tom forgot. Kisses
me hard against the closet

door in the hotel *want*
to skip the dance altogether
but I shake my head

you only get one senior prom you know.
We kiss the whole way down
in the elevator then make

our way to the dance floor.
Jordyn & Gretchen are there,
Gretchen's neckline spreading

in a wide V-neck. "Save Tonight"
is blasting in the ballroom, somewhere
between a slow song & a fast song

tomorrow comes with one desire
to take me away

Punch

I go get punch & Gretchen spikes it
from a silver flask in her bag

but before I can take a sip
I catch a glimpse of Jay Gatsby

rented tux, sallow eyes
he's standing by the door

to the lobby, watching me
like a hummingbird

I move so fast to stay in place
Tom catches me staring

what is with that guy he asks
& I shrug, I'm speechless

I'm gonna go talk to him Tom says
& I flash on the image

of him punching Jay's mouth
I'll come too & thankfully

Gretchen is listening
let's all go

Going Up

Daisy, Tom, Jay, Jordyn & Gretchen together in an elevator going up to the room to talk.

Didn't take much convincing.

Daisy.

What the fuck are you doing here?

What do you think I'm doing here?

Hey man, let's have a talk.

Yeah I think we've all got a lot to say.

Room

Before the hotel room seemed sleek, clean & private & anonymous
but now it seems like a sad blank slate, clichéd posters of the skyline.

I expect Tom to pelt Jay with questions but his first question is for me:
Do you want him here?

Not *who is he* not *do you love him* not *did you cheat* not *why*.
As if all that matters is this moment and the moments to come.

Do you want him here?

I can't help it; I start crying. My shoulders shaking,
tears coming down fast.
Jordyn puts an encouraging arm
around my waist.

Gretchen is studying Tom, trying to decide if he's dangerous.

He shouts this time. *DO YOU WANT HIM HERE?*

No. I shake my head. *No, Tom, no. I don't want him here.*

Tom swivels to face Jay. *Then why are you here?*

I—

Tom's pitch rising back up to a shout *IT WAS A RHETORICAL QUESTION, DUDE. YOU DO NOT GET TO TALK.*

Everybody calm down, Gretchen says, and I see that I have overestimated her powers.

Tom, I say, *I'm sorry, it's over, I was upset about—*

How well do you really know this guy? Tom cuts me off. *Oh yeah, I've been to the parties. You know how he pays rent? Pays for kegs?*

I nod, shame-faced. *I know he sells pot, Tom.*

Sells pot? Tom's laughing, now, a hyena, a crow. *SELLS POT? Oh, he sells pot all right.*
Sells a right lot of pot. Sells his ideas too, Daisy. Sells
his smarts. Did he tell you
he's available for hire? You know how he knows
all those kids at his parties, Daisy? He writes their papers for them.

Tom pauses, laughs, winks at Jay ironically.
Helped me out with my personal statement for Brown,
as a matter of fact. Thanks again, dude.

Suddenly nobody else
is in the room. I look
at Jay. *Why would you*
do that instead of going
to college yourself? I thought
that was the plan, thought
your parents had saved up.

He looks at me like the child
he so recently was. *Didn't*
graduate, Daze. I didn't graduate

Nelson. I was helping kids

with their papers there too

and got caught & expelled

but I'm glad, Daisy,

it was worth it to come here

to try to get you back.

Get you back? Nelson?

A new piece of the puzzle

clicks in for Tom.

Everybody calm down,

Gretchen says, *let's*

stay calm and talk

this out like adults

& Jordyn squeezes

my side, she is here

at least but no longer

can she protect me.

Daisy Tom turns to face me

behind one door we have a high-school

dropout—he pivots to Jay—*are you still*

a dropout if you got expelled? Well that's beside

the point. Behind one door you have a high-

school dropout selling pot

& selling essays to rich kids
to pay the rent while he basically
stalks you, behind the other door

you have Tom Buchanan & our history
and our future together in Providence
and we never have to talk about this creep

again. It's an easy choice but still
the tears are flowing *I choose you Tom*
want to stay with you forever

want to stay with you tonight in this room
and do everything & Tom laughs
yeah not happening tonight

Daisy I get a free pass tonight
I'm gonna get shitfaced & use
this room however I want

Tom pushes past me,
exits, and slams the door.
Opens it again, pulls

the valet ticket out of his pocket
and hands it to Jay

get her home safe to Daddy he spits
say your goodbyes

and he's gone. I crumple
on the bed. Jordyn's rubbing
my back Gretchen's petting

my hair. *Daisy it's OK we'll stay*
with you want to get room service
we can do anything you want

but I get myself together, shake
my head & stand. *I think we should do*
what Tom said. I look at Jay.

Can you drive me home?

Drive (II)

I've composed my face nobody in the lobby would even wonder.

We wait by the curb for the valet to pull the car around.

You shouldn't have come, I say.

To prom or to West Egg? Jay asks.

Probably both.

Wind in my dress, mesh layer against my fingertips the blue of deepest waters.

Car pulls up. I touch the hood. Tom's not here to bat my hand away.

They call me the submarine girl. I go down
but nothing touches me

I'm driving, I say.

Earthquake

Jay, sensitive like a seismometer, but my earthquake, my great event.

His knowledge of me

registered like a fault line

in Tom's cruel body,

that body moving away.

Each leaf on the tree quivered.

The bird, its ruby throat, was still,

still but for the small heart beating,

the rise and fall of each breath.

Green Light

We are silent as I drive
home. It is like a birth.
We go down through
the bowels of the city.
Every light is green. Foot
to the pedal I am driving
myself I am driving
this story. Don't think
about Jay silent beside
me don't think at all.
Take the exit for West
Egg. I'll drop Jay
at his house, say goodbye
cold as ice, take the car
wherever I want, maybe
all the way back to the city
maybe I'll just stay out
tonight driving. *Tonight,*
tonight. Tonight is the last
night I'll see Jay. Tonight
is the last night Tom will
spend on his own, or in
the arms of other girls.
Who needs to wait
until summer? *My husband*
Tom Buchanan. My strong
cruel husband. So what
if we're young we can
always break up still.
Mama & Daddy didn't

but that doesn't mean we
can't. Full moon is a green light
eclipsing me, winking, watching
me eclipse myself. Almost
at Gatsby's house. There's a girl
crossing the street ahead, jaywalking,
crossing at an odd angle maybe
she's stumbling maybe
she had too much to drink

Daisy.

She looks like Glasses Girl.

Daisy.

She *is* Glasses Girl, crossing
the street to her apartment.

Daisy.

Jay's voice is background noise,
white noise, a whisper.

Daisy.

Glasses Girl bends to adjust the heel
of her shoe, is it stuck between the stones
is it broken

DAISY!

Jay's screams sound very far away he grabs the wheel but it's too late

Swim Hole (II)

On the last Sunday of the Nelson School, Jay takes me to a swim hole

& after, our bodies wet, we walk, index fingers linked

until we find a clearing

& we lie

on our towels,   our eyes

closed against the sunlight

Hospital

Like coming to the surface of the water
I'm drowned but alive
Can't move
Can't speak
Can't open my eyes
But I can listen

A good prognosis all things considered

doesn't appear to have been under the influence of alcohol

And if she was? She wasn't the one driving.

I'm sorry sir I thought your daughter was the one driving

No it was the boy *That reckless murderous boy*

Sir do you know who we could reach

regarding him *No doctor I've never seen him before in my life*

He wasn't your daughter's prom date?

No doctor *certainly not we can't imagine why he had her*
boyfriend's car

Time

How long has it been?

hours, days weeks months centuries

I'm weak, I wake

Mama & Daddy watching over me

my room, my desk, my green lamp

What happened? Did I say that out loud or just think it?

Glasses Girl bending to touch her shoe

my eyes on her, my mind on her

until we melded into one.

Was it an accident? My brain forms the words but no sound comes out.

Mama shushes me but I can speak *What happened?*

You were in an accident dear. That boy hit a pedestrian.

But I was driving. I hit her.

Your memory's a little foggy. The boy was driving.

Tom . . .

Another boy had you in Tom's car, lord knows

why you left

with him, it doesn't matter now.

You rest. You rest today

& we'll discuss everything tomorrow.

Jay . . . is Jay OK?

You're not to mention that boy again.

Purity (II)

(petals)

(petals)(petals)

(petals)(petals)(petals)

(petals) (petals)

(petals)

S

T

E (petal, falling)

M

earth//earth//earth//earth

Erasure:
The Great Gatsby, Final Chapter

I remember that night as an endless drill of police and photographers

a rope stretched
across my body

grief in its simplest form:
I found myself alone

I called Daisy and no one answered the phone.
I felt a certain shame.
I should have known better.

the sky had turned dark, I was already too far
away

Daisy began to twinkle
Her hand, which dangles over the side, sparkles cold with jewels

For a transitory enchanted moment I thought of the light

Just a Girl (III)

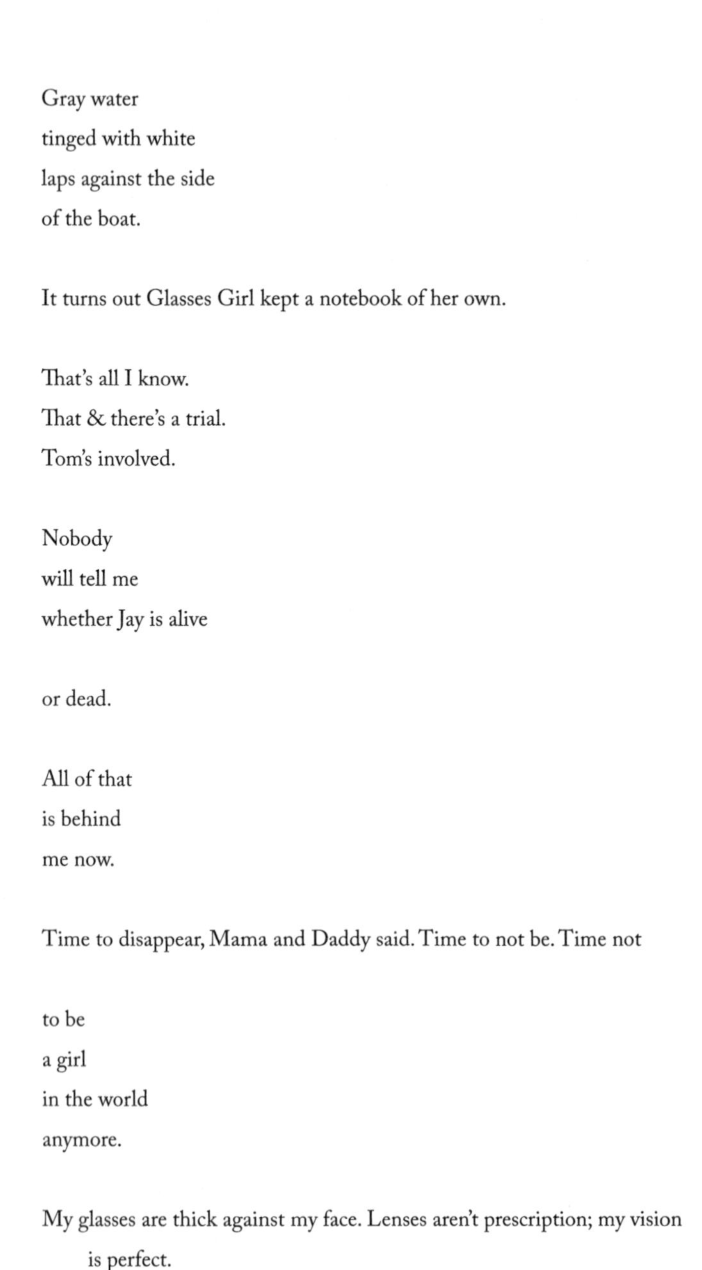

Gray water
tinged with white
laps against the side
of the boat.

It turns out Glasses Girl kept a notebook of her own.

That's all I know.
That & there's a trial.
Tom's involved.

Nobody
will tell me
whether Jay is alive

or dead.

All of that
is behind
me now.

Time to disappear, Mama and Daddy said. Time to not be. Time not

to be
a girl
in the world
anymore.

My glasses are thick against my face. Lenses aren't prescription; my vision
is perfect.

They're from a thrift store but then, they must have belonged to somebody's
grandfather.

I take them
off & drop them
over the railing.

They disappear
into the ocean
without making a splash.

My naked eyes trail the distant horizon. That's all I see now but soon
a new land will come into view.

Finger the passport folded
in my pocket. My new name
is another flower, deeper, aromatic.

Art school abroad? The very thing, Daddy.

Didn't let me say goodbye just had me write
a note in case the truth comes out.

Two questions I still can't answer:

Was it an accident?

Did I escape?

It's something for my poetry, anyway.
It's something to feel.

Myrtle, a blooming bush in which you can take shelter.

Myrtle, my roots creeping over the bones of the dead.

I rise like a phoenix from the valley of ashes.

My boat beats on against the current.

ACKNOWLEDGMENTS

Daisy would still be living in my head if my dad hadn't sent me an article about *The Great Gatsby* coming into the public domain, if McCormick Templeman hadn't said *drop everything and write it*, if Becky LeJeune hadn't responded with enthusiasm and read the book a dozen times and made it better, if Marisa Siegel hadn't seen immediately to the beating heart of the project and asked all the most probing questions, if my anonymous peer reviewer hadn't gone through an imaginary girl's juvenilia with a fine-toothed comb. Eleni Arapkiles and Adair Taylor were the brilliant high school English teachers who might remember me complaining about *Gatsby* et cetera and who I hope might one day read this book and know they taught me to sound the chasms in the literary canon. I am always so honored to do a book with Northwestern University Press and truly grateful to everyone on the team, among them Christopher Bigelow, adam bohannon, Anne Gendler, Charlotte Keathley, Greta Polo, Dino Robinson, Madeline Schultz, Courtney Smotherman, and Kristen Twardowski. Thank you for wrapping your hands around this weird little project and preserving Daisy's heart-shaped poems.

The Kerouac novel quoted in "Honey" and "Alley" is *Maggie Cassidy.*

Thanks and love to Rob and Andrea Feder, to Jed Feder and Tiffany Tatreau, to Nathaniel and Noah Kornfeld, and to Julia Michie Bruckner, boon companion in all the creative endeavors of this strange and beautiful middle season. This book is dedicated to Moshe Kornfeld with tremendous love, even though the first time he read it, he was like, *who are you.* And I'm grateful to Sierra Shaffer, who was with me in the expanded field of girlhood, and who will probably like this book best of all.